SECOND-GRADE DOG

Laurie Lawlor
Pictures by Gioia Fiammenghi

ALBERT WHITMAN & COMPANY
Niles, Illinois

Library of Congress Cataloging-in-Publication Data
Lawlor, Laurie.
Second-grade dog/Laurie Lawlor:
illustrated by Gioia Fiammenghi.
     p.   cm.
   Summary: Lonely Bones, the Mudheads' dog,
disguises himself as a second-grader and spends
an adventurous day at school.
ISBN 0-8075-7280-2 (lib. bdg.)
[1. Dogs—Fiction. 2. Schools—Fiction.
3. Humorous stories.]
I. Fiammenghi, Gioia, ill.
II. Title.
PZ7.L4189Se 1990   89-22700
[E]—dc20   CIP
                                          AC

Text © 1990 by Laurie Lawlor.
Illustrations © 1990 by Gioia Fiammenghi.
Designer: Karen Johnson Campbell.
Published in 1990 by Albert Whitman & Company,
5747 West Howard Street, Niles, Illinois 60648.
Published simultaneously in Canada by
General Publishing, Limited, Toronto.
Printed in the United States of America.
10 9 8 7 6 5 4 3 2 1

The text for this book is set in Italia Book.

For Boone. L.L.
For my children. G.F.

On Monday morning at precisely eight-thirty-one, Bones had a brilliant idea. He decided to become a second-grade dog.

There was nothing cruel or beastly about his owners, the Mudheads. They treated Bones with every kindness they could imagine. He was given the run of the house all day while they were at work. Bones could lounge on the best sofa, shred rolls of toilet paper, or howl at squirrels to his heart's content.

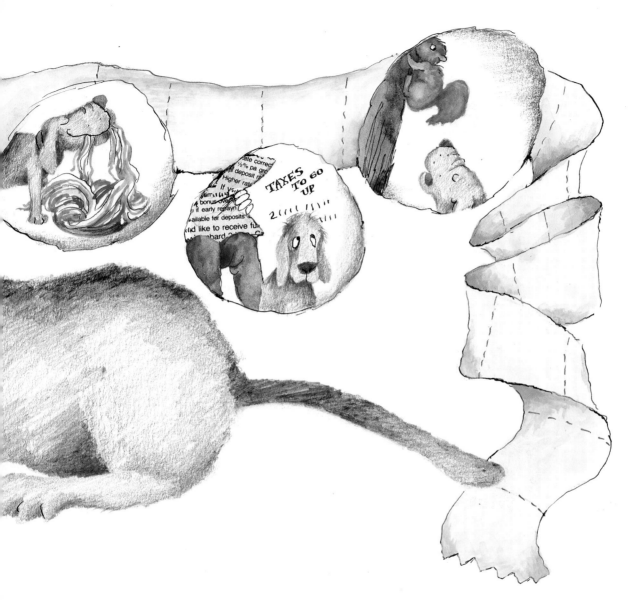

On his birthday, Mrs. Mudhead gave Bones a big plate of spaghetti. For entertainment, Mr. Mudhead read to Bones from the business section of the newspaper.

Although his owners were always very thoughtful, Bones was bored. Something important was missing from his life. Friends. Especially friends who knew how to have fun.

Every day Bones sat beside the front window where the burglars never came and looked out longingly at children as they walked to school. The children wore bright T-shirts and carried backpacks with dangling straps.

Sometimes they dragged big sticks. Sometimes they tossed balls. Sometimes they balanced on fire hydrants. Sometimes they ran and chased each other. How Bones wished he could play with them! He barked, but the children never stopped to chat.

"There's only one solution," Bones said to himself. "I'll disguise myself as a second grader and follow the children to school. Maybe then they'll be my friends."

Bones scrambled up to the attic, where Mrs. Mudhead stored boxes of old clothes. He sniffed. He found some outfits that had once belonged to the Mudheads' son, who was grown up and at college.

Tipping over several boxes, Bones pawed through piles of shirts. Some were too small. Some were too big. Finally, he dug up a T-shirt with a picture of a shark. The wonderful shirt fit!

Bones pulled on a pair of colorful shorts and peered in the mirror. He looked just like a second grader!

Now all he needed was a backpack. Bones tunneled his way
through boxes of Christmas tree decorations, baseball cards,
and old high school trophies. At last, he found exactly
what he was looking for. A red backpack with
dangling straps! He practiced slinging it
over his shoulder.

Because his paws were so large, Bones had trouble finding old sneakers that fit right. He searched and searched and finally picked out a bright orange pair. The rest of the afternoon, he practiced walking like a second grader.

Just before the Mudheads came home from work, Bones dashed downstairs and hid his disguise under the sofa. He hoped Mr. and Mrs. Mudhead would not notice the happy gleam in his eye and suspect he was up to something. Bones could hardly wait until tomorrow. As soon as his owners left, he would be on his way to school!

The next morning Bones lingered by the window until he heard children's voices. Slinging his backpack over his shoulder, he turned the knob of the unlocked door without any trouble. Boldly, he leaped over the fence and hurried out to the sidewalk. He had never jumped over the fence before and was a little out of breath. But no matter.

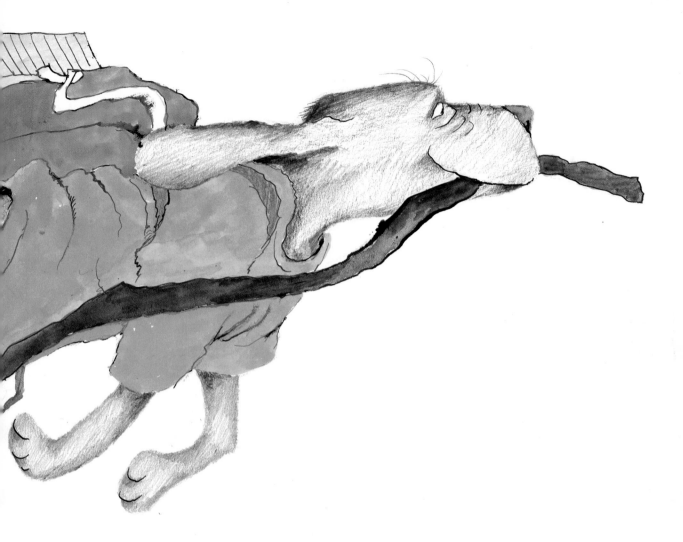

Bones fell in step behind two boys who were
having a sword fight with pencils as they walked
along. He was so excited to be going to school that
he forgot about his disguise. Grabbing an enormous
fallen branch in his mouth, he trotted between the
boys. Luckily, neither of them thought Bones was
acting the least bit strange.

"Look at his weapon!" one boy shouted. The
other laughed and chased Bones all the way to school.

Before he reached the school gate, Bones dropped the big branch for the boys to share. He stood up on two feet like a second grader, brushed himself off, and decided to explore the noisy playground. Children were everywhere, swinging and sliding and jumping rope. Bones was thrilled. "I'm sure I can find someone here who will be my friend," he thought.

Suddenly, a soccer ball flew through the air and landed nearby. "Over here! Over here!" yelled a group of kids.

Bones gave the ball a swift kick, and it went flying. He was very pleased. He had never realized he was good at sports.

"Hey, who's the new kid?" someone shouted.

"He's on our team!" a tall boy replied.

With Bones' help, two goals were quickly scored.

"We won! We won!" his teammates shouted. They surrounded Bones and jumped up and down. He joined in happily, barking and wagging his tail.

The kids were delighted to find out that Bones was really a dog.

"Good work!" said a boy from the game. He winked at Bones. "My name is Nick. Mrs. Lampshade's second-grade class could sure use somebody like you!"

The bell rang. "We'd better hurry," Nick said to Bones. "Just follow me." Nick ran toward the door.

Bones gladly followed Nick up the steps through the stampede of legs. School was filled with marvelous smells—baloney, mop soap, chalk dust, gym socks. But there was no time to explore. Bones had to keep his nose in the direction his new friend was going.

They walked into Room 213, and Bones took an empty seat behind Nick. The desk was a bit of a squeeze.

"Good morning, class," said Mrs. Lampshade.

Bones sat straight and tall. He did not fidget. He did not want to get into trouble on his first day of school.

"And who are you?" Mrs. Lampshade asked Bones after she had called roll.

"He's the new kid," Nick said quickly.

"Yeah, he just came to this country," another second grader explained helpfully, grinning all the while.

"And he doesn't know any English yet," Nick added.

Mrs. Lampshade, who was very nearsighted, wiped her thick glasses. "All right, then. Go down the hall to the English language class. Nick, show our new student the way. The rest of you please open your math books."

Bones was glad to escape from Mrs. Lampshade's class. Math was his worst subject.

He sat down in the back of the special English classroom.
Bones was in luck. The class was up for grabs because Mr.
Pencilshaving had lost his voice. Students wandered in and out.
Paper airplanes soared through the air. Mr. Pencilshaving tried
whispering and waving his arms, but the only one paying
attention was Bones. Bones sat politely while a girl from Japan
recited the Pledge of Allegiance to the flag. The girl was so
pleased by his attention that she gave him a green pencil eraser.
Bones thought the eraser was very tasty.

Next came art. Bones was quite a painter. The art teacher stopped to admire him at work. "Be creative, class!" said Miss Adhesivetape, who always dressed in an interesting way. Today she was wearing a paper bag over her head.

Bones covered his entire canvas with bold swipes of blue and black and red. Expertly, he shredded bits of tissue and pressed them here and there. The effect was stunning.

The class cheered.

Bones was very modest. He did not howl or strut proudly around the room. He refused to let artistic success go to his head.

The lunch bell rang. Bones followed the crowd to the lunchroom. He looked in his backpack, but he'd forgotten to bring something to eat.

"Don't worry. You can share my lunch," said Nick. He handed Bones half a peanut-butter sandwich. The other kids at the table gave Bones raisins, a bag of corn chips, two cartons of milk, a carton of yogurt, and a banana.

What a big meal! Bones wished he could take a nap. But there was no time. He had to hurry to Mrs. Lampshade's language arts class.

While Mrs. Lampshade droned on and on about this week's spelling words, Bones daydreamed about the Mudheads' nice, soft sofa. RRRRRRRR-ing! RRRRRRRR-ing! Bones sat up straight when he heard the sudden loud bell.

"We're having a fire drill!" someone called out. "No spelling quiz today!"

"Hooray!" the class yelled.

Mrs. Lampshade's students filed outside. Soon the whole school was lined up neatly around the playground fence. Bones stood stiffly, trying not to think about how tight his sneakers felt.

The city fire marshal and Mr. Paperclip, the principal, marched past. The fire marshal stopped. Bones held his breath.

"Does everything seem to be in order?" Mr. Paperclip asked nervously. He did not want anything to go wrong. He was proud of his school's perfect fire drill record.

"Hmmm," replied the city fire marshal, who was very strict and proper at all times.

Carefully, he inspected the children to make sure none of them whispered or chewed gum or wore their shoelaces untied. "Say, what's this?" he asked suddenly.

"What's what?" asked Mr. Paperclip.

"Did you know that you have a dog in your school? That's against the rules."

"A dog?" Mr. Paperclip said, quite shocked.

"A dog?" squeaked Mrs. Lampshade.

"A dog?" rasped Mr. Pencilshaving.

"A dog?" mumbled Miss Adhesivetape.

"There's no dog!" Nick and the other second graders insisted.

"Oh, yes there is. And he's right there." The city fire marshal pointed to Bones.

Bones hung his head.

"No dogs are permitted at any time on school grounds by order of the Board of Education of District Seventy-Five," the city fire marshal announced. "Page forty-seven, rule number six hundred thirty-one."

"Is it true this dog is in *your* class, Mrs. Lampshade?" Mr. Paperclip said crossly.

"I thought he was a new student," Mrs. Lampshade replied, her voice trembling.

The city fire marshal scowled at Mr. Paperclip, who scowled at Mrs. Lampshade, who scowled at Bones. Mrs. Lampshade shook her finger. "Bad dog!" she said. "Go home!"

Bones dropped miserably on all fours and tucked his tail between his legs.

Nick and the other second graders did not want Bones sent away. "Unfair! Unfair! Unfair!" they chanted.

It wasn't long before the rest of the school joined in. "Unfair! Unfair!" their voices echoed. The noise was so loud that the neighbors peered out of windows. People stopped their cars and stared.

"Goodness, gracious!" Mrs. Lampshade said.

"This unlawful disturbance will have to stop!" the city fire marshal said. "Do something, Mr. Paperclip!"

The principal looked embarrassed. What should he do? Allowing Bones to stay would set a terrible example. The next thing he knew, he might have to deal with cats, parakeets, guinea pigs, snakes, and turtles roaming the school halls. No, he had to be firm. "I'm sorry. Rules are rules. This dog must leave."

Sadly, Bones picked up his backpack and began walking home.

"If he goes, I go!" Nick announced.

"Me, too! Me, too!" said everyone else in Mrs. Lampshade's class. Instantly, the entire second grade galloped down the street behind Bones.

"Come back!" squeaked Mrs. Lampshade.

"Come back!" rasped Mr. Pencilshaving.

"Come back!" mumbled Miss Adhesivetape.

"Come back!" bellowed Mr. Paperclip.

"Come back!" commanded the city fire marshal.

But Nick and the other second graders were already out of sight.

They followed Bones to the Mudheads' house. For the rest of the afternoon, they ate snacks and played soccer. Nick organized a game of tag, and Bones showed everyone how to jump over the fence. The children threw balls for Bones. They challenged him to tug of war. Finally, everyone collapsed in front of the television.

"I can't believe it's time to go home," Nick told Bones. "Can all of us come and visit tomorrow after school?"

Bones joyfully barked and wagged his tail.

"Great! We'll see you then," Nick said.

"Goodbye!" the other children said. They waved and hurried on their way.

That evening the Mudheads came home from work
before Bones could clean up the mess or hide his
disguise. Mr. and Mrs. Mudhead were surprised
to find the refrigerator nearly empty, muddy
footprints everywhere, and the television blaring.
"And look at that wild shirt and shorts Bones
is wearing!" Mrs. Mudhead exclaimed.
"The poor dog! He's not at all himself.
Why don't we order some take-out spaghetti
to see if that will help bring him back
to normal?" Mr. Mudhead suggested.
"Good idea," replied his wife.
Bones smacked his lips.
When the spaghetti
came, he ate
every last noodle.

Being in second grade had not turned out quite
the way Bones had planned. But no matter. He had
enjoyed himself tremendously. Snuggled on the sofa
between Mr. and Mrs. Mudhead, Bones sighed with
contentment. Life was certainly not boring anymore.

He dozed off, imagining all the fun he'd have tomorrow with Nick and his new friends. In his sleep, Bones thumped his tail and paddled one paw back and forth, back and forth. And why not? Bones was dreaming. He was zooming down the street again with the entire second grade behind him. Only this time, they were all riding skateboards.